Bedtime
for little
dragons

by Irene Yates
illustrated by Helen Floate

D1134555

Ladybird

In the dragons' cave it's...
get-ready-for-bed-time.

Mummy Dragon says,

*"Come on, little dragons,
it's time to clear away.
Pick up all your toys and things,
it's the end of the day!"*

And Little Baby Dragon says,

"day-day-day!"

In the dragons' cave it's…
let's-have-a-bath-time.

Little Tom Dragon says,

"Come on, everybody!
Upstairs in a flash.
Who'll be in the water first?
Splish! Splosh! Splash!"

And Little Baby Dragon says,

"splish! splosh! splash!"

In the dragons' cave it's…
jump-into-jim-jams-time.

Mummy Dragon says,

"Vest and jim-jams! Quickly!
Cover up those tums!
Let's get you ready for your beds
before your daddy comes!"

And Little Baby Dragon says,

"comes.comes
'comes!"

In the dragons' cave it's…
goodnight-drink-and-biscuit-time.

Little Jack Dragon says,

"I want a crunchy biscuit —
one with chocolate on the top!
I'm going to have my mug of milk,
and drink up every drop."

And Little Baby Dragon says,

"drop-drop-drop!"

In the dragons' cave it's…
let's-clean-your-teeth-time.

Daddy Dragon says,

*"Brush those teeth till they
glitter and gleam.
Then bounce into bed to
dream dragon dreams!"*

And Little Baby Dragon says,

"dreams-dreams-dreams!"

In the dragons' cave it's…
curl-up-for-a-story-time.

Daddy Dragon says,

"Once upon a time
in a faraway land,
there was a little magic boy
who built a castle out of sand."

And Little Baby Dragon says,

"sand, sand, sand!"

In the dragons' cave it's...
snuggle-down-to-sleep-time.

Mummy and Daddy Dragon say,

"Night, night, sleep tight,
it's time for us to put out the light."

They wait a while but don't
hear a peep – for the little dragons
are...

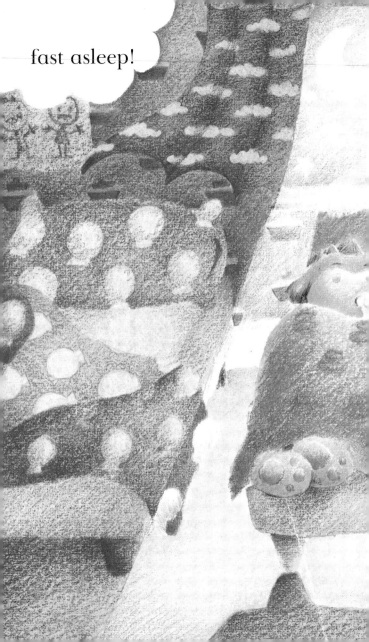

fast asleep!

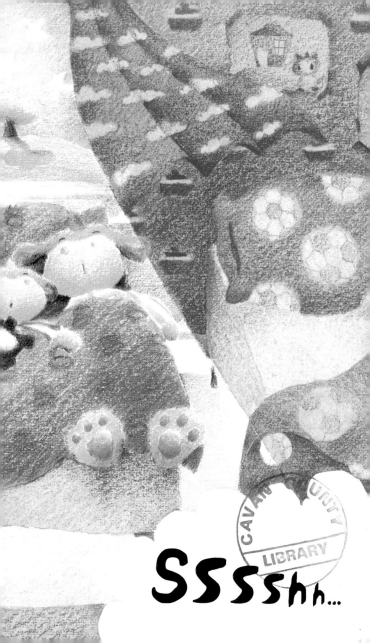

SSSShh...